My Dinosaur Is Scared Of Vegetables

Lily Lexington

IMPROVIGY PTY LTD
• SYDNEY, AUSTRALIA •

ISBN-13: 978-1479333462
ISBN-10: 1479333468

Jack, in the closet, was hiding from Mom.
His dinosaur whimpered and sucked on his thumb.
It was time for their dinner and there was no way,
They'd EVER eat their vegetables, not on THIS day.

"Jack, come out, it's time for your dinner.
Who can eat faster? I bet you're the winner."
"Mom, I'm afraid that I have to stay here.
My dinosaur's shaking and trembling with fear.

He's frightened of carrots and broccoli and peas,
Beetroots and squash cause the poor beast to sneeze.
They will destroy him with one single bite,
That is the reason he stays out of sight."

"I see." said Jack's mother, "I guess then instead.
"Your dinosaur promptly must go straight to bed.
There he will so much further away
From the vegetable dishes we're eating today."

Jack feeling angry decided right then,
To go to his room with his dinosaur friend.
He stomped up the stairs and then slammed his door.
"I don't even care if I eat anymore.
I can still play and I can have fun,
I don't need those vegies to be number one!"

The very next morning Jack happily said,
"Today is a great day to get out of bed!
A cool game like baseball is always such fun,
I almost can't wait till I hit a homerun!"

The dinosaur followed Jack into the kitchen,
Where they both realized that something was missing.
"Where is my breakfast?" Jack noisily said.
'Cause there on the table sat vegies instead.

His dinosaur ran to the family room table,
And hid underneath as best he was able.
"Jack, you will eat all these vegetables now."
His mother exclaimed as he put his head down.

But Jack turned around and said, "There's, No Way!
My dinosaur's still scared of vegies, OK?"

They got in the car and drove to the park,
The dinosaur jumped when he heard a dog bark.
Jack's Mom ignored him, her face wore a frown,
While Jack got his gear on she sat on the ground.

Jack's dino was tired, he got up and yawned.
Then sat on the bench at the side of the lawn.
The game soon began, with Jack up to bat,
He swung! Strike ONE, and adjusted his hat.

Another, Strike TWO, Jack missed the ball!
Jack was not swinging his bat well at all.

The third pitch came then and Jack swung at the ball
"Three Strikes, you're out!" came the umpire's call.
Out to the field the players had run.
But Jack of course was having no fun.

His dinosaur snoozed, his eyes tired and bleary.
Jack stood mid field feeling heavy and weary.

The ball flew towards him, he went for the catch.
But he tripped and he fell and he lost the whole match!

The game was now ended but Jack didn’t know,
Why he was tired and being so slow.
His dinosaur nudged him as if he should say,
“I’m terribly sorry you’ve had a bad day.”

Jack’s mother bundled them into the car
And soon they were home as the park wasn’t far.

His mother smiled kindly, “Jack may I please,
Talk with your dinosaur out by the trees?”
So Jack waited patiently, too tired to walk.
While Dino and Mom had a serious talk.

“We’ve had a good chat and we need you to know,
That we’ve figured out why today you were slow.”
The dinosaur smiled as Jack’s mother explained,
“Vitamins stop you from feeling so drained.”

Jack wrinkled his brow, “I don’t understand.”
“Are vitamins magic?” he held out his hand.
Mom put a carrot right into Jack’s palm,
And to his surprise his dino stayed calm.

"Vegetables help you to stay fast and strong,
Your dinosaur knows he was terribly wrong.
He's no longer frightened and trembling you see.
He's even agreed to try broccoli and peas."

Jack took a bite from the carrot and said
“This isn’t half bad,” and bit off its head.
From that day on the best friends knew,
That eating their vegies was something they’d do.

To stay strong and healthy in every which way,
They would eat vegetables every day.

A Note from the Author

To my dear readers:

Thank you so much for purchasing *My Dinosaur is Scared of Vegetables*. I really hope you and your kids enjoyed reading it as much I enjoyed writing it.

I appreciate that you chose to buy and read my book over some of the others out there. Thank you for putting your faith in me to help educate and entertain your children.

If you and your kids enjoyed *My Dinosaur is Scared of Vegetables* and you have a spare couple of minutes now, it would really help me out it if you would like to leave me a great review (even if it's brief) on Amazon. All these reviews really help me spread the word about my books and encourage me to write more and add more to the series!

If you'd like to read another one of the books from my Children's Books series, I've included some on the next page for you.

Warmest Regards,

Lily Lexington

Rhyming Books by Lily Lexington

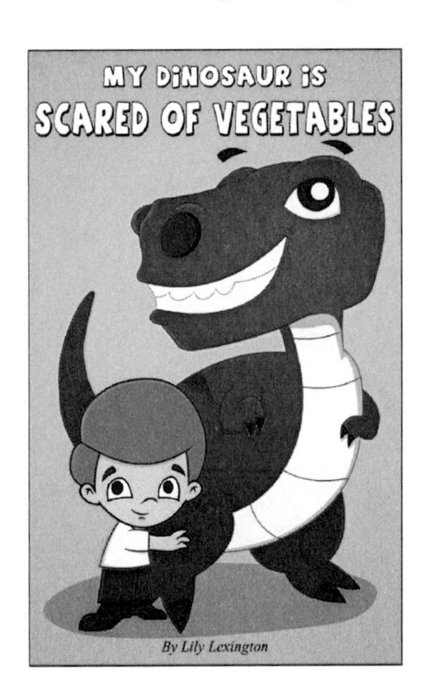

My Dinosaur is Scared of Vegetables

If you like stories by Maurice Sendak, Jon Klassen, Dr Seuss and P D Eastman then you will love this beautiful tale told by Lily Lexington in her debut children's story.

Follow Jack and his cute dinosaur friend in his quest to avoid eating his vegetables.

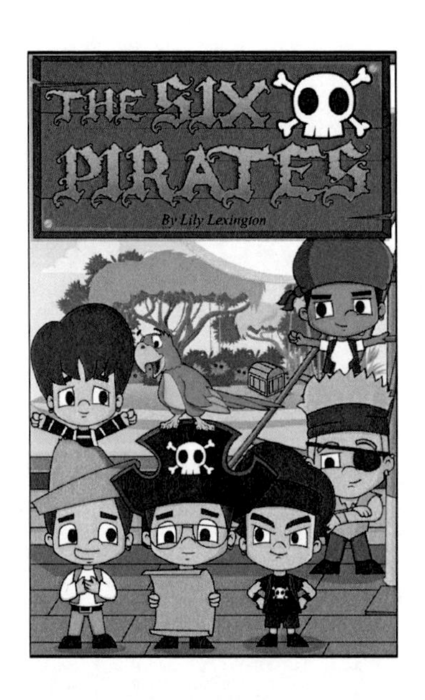

The Six Pirates:
A Rollicking and Rhyming Picture Book

If your child enjoys stories from authors like Jane Yolen, Kevin Henkes, Katherine Paterson or Patricia Polacco then your child will love this rollicking and rhyming sea adventure.

The six pirates have two big problems; they have run out of food and none of them can agree on where they should sail, let alone anything else. Will this be the end of the beloved six pirates or will the bickering buccaneers find their way to a new home?

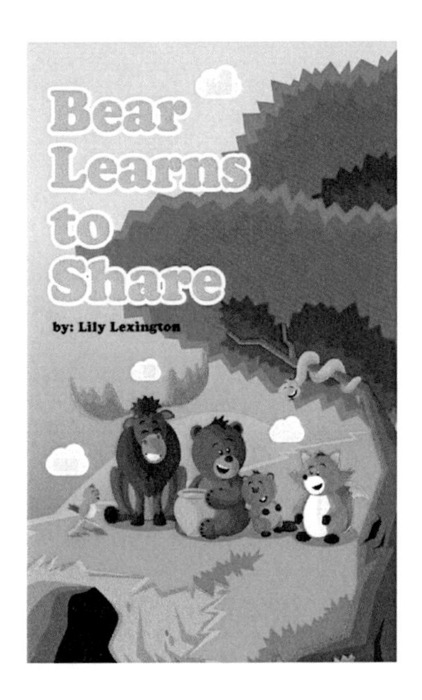

Bear Learns to Share

If your child enjoys stories like Winnie the Pooh or other stories by Maurice Sendak, Jon Klassen, Dr Seuss and P D Eastman then you will love this beautiful tale told by Lily Lexington in this children's story for kids both big and small.

Follow Bear with vibrant, colorful pictures as he plays with his friends in the forest and discovers what happens when he does not share.

Lola the Mermaid
and The Splish Splash Olympics

If your child enjoys stories from authors like Kate DiCamillo, Cynthia Rylant, Mem Fox or Gary Paulson then your child will love this beautiful mermaid tale told by Lily Lexington in this children's picture story book complete with a valuable lesson.

Follow Lola the Mermaid with beautiful illustrations in her quest to win the gold medal for diving in the Splish Splash Olympics. Will she win the gold medal? Discover what happens in this fun tale.

My Dad Is A Superhero

Does your dad have x-ray vision or can he fly faster than a speeding bullet?

5 year old Sam is not like other boys, at least not with respect to his father, who is a superhero. "My Dad is a Superhero" is a fun tale that explores Sam's bond with his dad and his incredible super powers.

Told from the point of view of Sam, it is a fun story that ends on a warm fuzzy note that is just perfect for bedtime. Children will take delight in the amazing and varied super powers of Sam's dad and parents will take delight in some of the humor placed throughout the tale.

This book is a bedtime story for ages 2-6.

Pick up your copy today!

The Tale of
Luna the Moth

Luna feels different from her butterfly family. She wants to belong but deep down she knows she is not the same as the other butterflies. Follow Luna in her journey to find out who she is in the cute story for kids both young and old.

The story ends with a great lesson about acceptance that all parents will resonate with.
- Beautiful, color illustrations that will captivate your young child.
- Rhyming lines help engage your child and sustain interest

Your younger children will enjoy the illustrations and sing-song tone of the story while your older children will particularly like the rhyming story format.

Book Availability

All of Lily's print books are available in digital format on the Amazon Kindle. Just go to your country specific Amazon website and search for Lily Lexington.

Lily's Works Translated

Lily's bestselling book; 'My Dad is a Superhero' has been translated into Spanish, German, French, Italian, Japanese and Portuguese. All of these books are available in digital version only on Amazon Kindle. To find them search for Lily Lexington on Amazon.com and browse through Lily's collection.